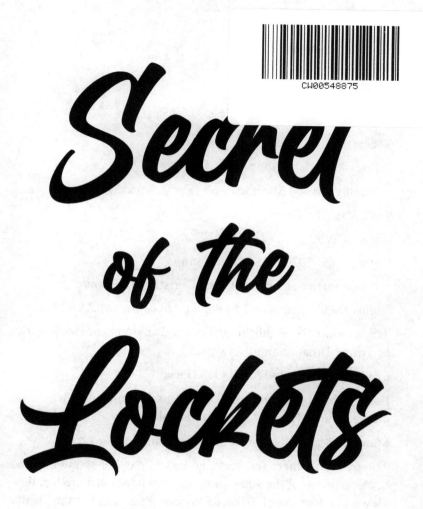

Secret of the Lockets

BY SHARON YOUNG

Secret of the Lockets

Trilogy Christian Publishers

A Wholly Owned Subsidiary of Trinity Broadcasting Network

2442 Michelle Drive

Tustin, CA 92780

For information, address Trilogy Christian Publishing

Rights Department, 2442 Michelle Drive, Tustin, CA 92780.

Trilogy Christian Publishing/ TBN and colophon are trademarks of Trinity Broadcasting Network.

Cover illustration by: Mary Och Gates

For information about special discounts for bulk purchases, please contact Trilogy Christian Publishing.

Manufactured in the United States of America

Trilogy Disclaimer: The views and content expressed in this book are those of the author and may not necessarily reflect the views and doctrine of Trilogy Christian Publishing or the Trinity Broadcasting Network.

10 9 8 7 6 5 4 3 2 1

Library of Congress Cataloging-in-Publication Data is available.

ISBN: 979-8-88738-161-9

ISBN: 979-8-88738-162-6

This book is dedicated to my family who have supported the idea behind the writing of this book, and to anyone who has a special dream no matter your age.

A gift to my grandchildren:
Jordan, Maliha, Anthony, Annalise, and Andrea

This is a fictional story based on loss, family,
and the faithfulness of God.

Chapter 1

The bright summer sun shone through the back glass of her car as she pulled onto the interstate heading anywhere but where she is at this moment. She could not have imagined this happening to her worst enemy.

She is Sidney Denise Sharpe, daughter to one of the town's local attorneys. Right after graduation she married the most wonderful man, Matthew Randall Livingston III, or so she thought. At the age of forty-five, she had returned to her hometown to make arrangements for her mother's funeral. Her father had died a few years earlier and being the only child, well you understand. The funeral service was nice and went well. It was good to see old friends and their children since she had lived away and did not return home as often as she should have. Although, she did enjoy her life in Atlanta with Matthew Randall Livingston, III Attorney at Law.

She changed out of my basic black dress and into some jeans and t-shirt and headed downstairs to begin the clean-up process. Her mother was well liked in our town, and she was known as a very friendly women, so there were lots of people wanting to help, but Sidney just needed this time to herself and in hopes that Matthew would help and that would give us time to spend together discussing what they would do with the property my parents had left me. Was she ever surprised when Matthew came into the kitchen where she had started loading the dishwasher and said, "Sid, I really need to discuss something with you." Sidney replied, "Let me finish loading the dishwasher and I will fix us a cup of coffee and we can have a nice long talk?" Much to her surprise Matthew blurted out, "I want a divorce. I am so sorry Sidney. I just can't hold it in any longer and I know that this may not be the right time, but now that I have said it, I feel like the weight of the world is off my shoulders. I have wanted to tell you this for months, but I just didn't know how too we have been together for all most seventeen years, and I love you as a friend and you are one amazing women, but I am not in love with you anymore."

That's a day she would never forget, but it was also the first day of a new beginning. Sidney picked herself up and focused on what she wanted to do with the rest of her life, for the first time she was truly on her own. She had no immediate family. No one to question her ideas and no one to answer to. Between her divorce settlement from Matthew, which was more than fair, and the estate her parents had left her, let's just say money was not a concern and the world was wide open. She would spend the next few weeks making arrangement to have all her personal things placed into storage and to sell her parents' home. Now to start planning a new future.

Sidney spent all her life on the East Coast which she loved very much, the Southern foods she had been raised on and the opportunity to experience the four seasons each year, from spring to the hottest summers through to the leaves changing colors and falling in autumn and even the coldest of snowing winters. As much as she would miss these things and with tear filled eyes of the childhood memories, she also knew it was time to move on and say good-bye.

The million-dollar question was: where to go? Where would she most like to live and start a new, wonderful, life for herself?

With movers running around from room to room packing items, some to be sent to storage while other items are on their way in hopes of being a helpful to others and bring a smile to some needy person's face. Sidney knew that her mother would have wanted her stuff given to someone who could really use the items. It about four weeks of steady everyday cleaning and organizing all the items throughout the house and deciding what she would want to keep and what she would give away. Now that the house has been sold and all affairs are in order, it was time for her to move on and close this chapter of my life.

As she made her way to the front door, she could hear the taxi cab as it pulled up in front of the house and as she reached for the door knob all her childhood memories came rushing back like, her first day of school, Mom with tears in her eyes and telling her that it was nothing, then the day Sidney came running down the stairs and rushing out the front door because Dad was waiting to take her to get her driver's license. Then Sidney could see her first date standing at the bottom of the stairs shaking in his shoes as her dad questioned him, and finally the day she walked down the stairs in her wedding dress. So many new beginnings took place in this very spot that it only seemed fitting that this be the same place that she would make her exit from this part of her life and head into her new beginnings.

Chapter 2

As the plane touched down, Sidney is suddenly overcome by fear as well an excitement and joy of the thought of starting a new life, meeting new people, and visiting new places. *The first thing I should do is head to the hotel and freshen up, check the time, and contact the real estate agent I had spoken with over the phone to see when we should start looking for a new place to call home.*

As she made her way through the airport, headed to the baggage claim area, she can't believe how many people are rushing through there. As she stands waiting for her bags to come through the conveyer belt, she can't help but notice a lovely gray-haired lady standing all alone. There comes one of my bags now, and as I reach down to pick the bag up; I suddenly feel another hand on mine. It's the grey-haired lady. "I am sorry." She said, "I thought that was my bag, I have one just like it." Sidney turned to say, "That is okay." She noticed that she has the kindest eyes and warmest smile. Then Sidney introduced herself, "Hi, my name is Sidney Sharpe, but my friends call me Sid, I am new to this part of the country I am from the East Coast, and I have decided to relocate to the West Coast, since I have always heard so much about it." With a soft voice she says, "Very glad to meet you, Sid. My name is Emma Grace Sterling, and my friends call me Emmy. Welcome to the West Coast I have lived here all my life; I have been visiting friends in Colorado." After a few minutes of waiting to claim all our baggage, they were on their way and as they walked through the airport for some odd reason, Sidney found myself being drawn to the grey-haired lady known as Emmy, *maybe because I missed my mother*. As they exited the doors to get into their taxi cabs, she handed Sidney a small piece of paper and said, "If you need anything give me a call."

She had checked into my hotel and just finished unpacking a few things stepped onto the balcony to look at the beautiful sun filled city below and reached for my date book to get the number for the New Harvest Real Estate Agency, the first thing that fell out was the piece of paper that Emmy had placed in her hand at the airport with her telephone number written on it. Sidney had this overwhelming need to call and let her know that she had made it to my hotel safely and that everything was okay. Before she knew it, she had dialed the number and this soft gentle voice answered saying, "Hello, is that you Sid? I had a feeling you would be calling." "Yes, ma'am it's me; but how did you know that I would call?" "Somethings you just know." She replied. "I just wanted to tell you I made it to my hotel safely and all is well. I am going to contact the real estate company and set up an appointment with them to start looking for a home." But almost before she could finish her sentence, Emmy jumped in and said, "Before you do that please come and visit with me, there will be time for that tomorrow, do you have a pen? Here is my address 778 Matthew Lane, I will see you within the hour, okay?"

Sidney responded, "Okay, that sounds nice I will see you then." She had never before been so taken with someone, but she seemed to be drawn to her kindness and genuine concern. After all, this was new beginnings, making new friends, and Emmy was her first new friend.

As she climbed into the cab the driver asked, "Where to Miss?" I replied, "Do you know where 778 Matthew Lane is?" He kind of chuckled and said, "Everyone knows where 778 Matthew Lane is you must not be from around here." She replied, "I am originally from the East Coast. I have decided to move here, so if you don't mind you can take your time as I would like to look around as we drive through town I am in no hurry."

As the taxi moved through the streets there were lovely shops, a coffee house, and a bookstore. The view was breath taking. They turned along a small cobble stone street and the view of the vineyards was the most wonderful site clusters of grapes on all the vines in every color you could think of. She asked the driver if they were almost there because she had not seen any houses since they turned onto the cobblestone street. He replied, "We are on Matthew Lane the house is up ahead." As she looked ahead, she noticed two large iron gates that had iron clusters of grapes within and what looked like a large scroll ribbon with the words *New Harvest Manor*. "There must be some mistake. Are you sure this 778 Matthew Lane?" And once again, he said, "I am sure, everyone knows where 778 Matthew Lane is." As he pulled to the front door; Sidney saw Miss Emmy standing on the porch and she waved happily. She paid the taxi driver and thanked him once again for the little tour he gave along the way too Emmy's house.

"So glad to see you again dear, I hope your ride here was pleasant." "The scenery was beautiful, is this your home? It is beautiful beyond words." "Dear, I have lived here all my life and couldn't imagine being anywhere else. It is magical. I will give you a tour and a little history later, now first things first. I would like you to meet the man in my life, my companion who loves me unconditionally." She called out the name, "Levi!" "Levi, we have a guest I would like you to meet, where are you?" Down the staircase, the most beautiful Australian Sheppard appears. He sits at her feet, and she introduces us, "Levi, this is Sidney and Sidney this is Levi." He then lifted his left paw as to say, 'nice to meet you' and Sidney reached down to shake his paw and said, "Very nice to meet you." He kissed the back of her hand. Sidney says, "What a nice dog you have." "Are you an animal lover?" Emmy asked her. "Oh I love dogs, maybe once I am settled in, I can think about getting a dog of my own"

Just then a nicely dressed gentlemen entered the room. "Sidney, this is Jed McAdams, he is caretaker here and knows everything there is to know about our town, if you need help with anything please feel free to ask him." "Yes." Jed agrees and says, "Very nice to make your acquaintance Miss Sidney." "But how did you know my name was Sidney?" "Miss Emmy told me all about you when I picked her up from the airport." "Oh! I see." She said. "Jed, could you have some refreshments brought to the back patio for us while we sit and have a nice long visit?" "Yes, Miss Emmy, right away." "Thank you." Emmy replied.

Chapter 3

Sidney said, "The view of the mountains is unbelievable from this room." "It is." replied Emmy. "That was one of the main reasons my Great-Great Grandfather Alex Ross Sterling built New Harvest Manor in this spot, the views are breath taking and there is a sense of peace sitting here and looking over the land. I will take you on a tour of the gardens and give you a small history lesson on the town of New Harvest and just how she got started."

"Great-Great Grandfather was very much the entrepreneur in his day and while visiting the area fell in love with the views of the mountains and surrounding area. He lived in a time when towns would pop up wherever the people decided to settle. In order to make his dreams come true he knew that he would need to help other people make their dreams come true as well. Life is so rewarding and blessed when you help your neighbor, don't you agree?" "Yes ma'am." Sidney replied. "He sent out information letting people know that he was building a home and starting a winery and that there would be jobs available, and men began to come to the area. The men loved the area so much they decided to stay. Soon the families began arriving and the town began. Great-Great Grandfather helped many of the women open local shops for selling goods that would be needed for everyday life, while their husbands worked in the vineyards, or building whatever their craft or talent was, they were given the choice to pick whatever they felt they were best at. You know we all have been given a talent we just have to figure out what it is. Then New Harvest the town was born, the vines produce a new harvest of grapes each year. Great-Great Grandfather would say that a new harvest means we can begin a new and it was new beginnings for the people that moved to the area.

His son was Alex Ross Sterling II which was my Great-Grandfather and his son, Alex Ross Sterling III, was my grandfather and that brings us to my Father Alex Ross Sterling IV.

All the men in my family were very business minded and good at finances and investments. Each generation seemed to look out for the generation after them, to preserve and protect, so that the next generation could enjoy things also. Things are so different in this day and time. Don't you agree? All the men in my family were loving and caring men; they had great reputations and were well liked in town.

My father Alex Ross Sterling IV met Mary Grace Dowell while attending college in the East and after graduation my father knew he would always come back to New Harvest. Mary Grace decided to pay him a visit and she was mesmerized with the town, soon after they were engaged and even married here on the grounds of the winery. My mother was a veterinarian and opened a small animal clinic and my dad, of course, came and worked the winery and learned everything he could because he knew one day he would take over as the owner. It seemed that every generation, until now, had been blessed with a son. Mom and Dad were blessed with me and with the hopes of eventually having a son. They did not give me the name of Alex, they named me after my mother's, mother. Whatever the reason, they never did have any other children, but dad always said that it was okay not having a son because I was the twinkle in his eye. My parents were the best; I had a wonderful childhood. My mom blessed me with love for animals and dad for the love of the land."

"Does that mean your father and mother attended college on the east coast?" "They both attended the University of North Carolina, and my mother was from a small town in North Carolina. I never really have known anyone from her side of the family, her parents died when she was in grade school, and she didn't seem to have many memories after the car accident they were in. At the time she was around ten or eleven, the only thing she ever said was that she had a vague memory of a baby, but she was raised in an orphanage, and we never talked any further about her childhood, she always said she was blessed with a wonderful life and God new what he was doing."

By this time, several hours had passed by. Sidney had been swept up in Emmy's story. *It would be dinner time soon and I should be making my way back to the hotel.* "Emmy your family has so much history. I would love to hear more, but maybe I should get back to the hotel and let you get some rest." "Nonsense." Emmy replied, "The time to rest will come later in life. I have the most wonderful idea, why don't you stay here with me for a while, I have plenty of room and you would be great company for me. That will give you the chance to learn more about our town and the people who live here and to figure out what it is you would like to do and live.

"I'll have Jed drive you to the hotel to pick up your bags and when you come back, we'll have dinner and chat to our hearts content. What do you say Sidney? Will you stay with us? Levi and I would love to have you here! Say yes!" "It is a wonderful place to be, and I am so enjoying your friendship and I feel so at home here, are you sure?" "YES!" "Okay I would love to be your guest."

As Jed's car left the driveway headed to the hotel, Sidney wondered what she was thinking, *I hardly know this lady, but yet I feel so at ease with her and even drawn to her in a way I can't explain.*

Chapter 4

"Thanks so much Emmy for helping me get settled in, this is a lovely room the lavender and cream colors are so calming and peaceful." "This room originally was a sewing room used by my late Grandmother and since I cannot sew a lick as they say! I decided to redecorate the room; somehow, I knew you would just love it. Dinner should be ready soon, I bet you are starting to get a bit hungry; I know that I am.," said Emmy as they made our way down the stairs. "I believe we are having roast chicken with steamed vegetables." "Sounds wonderful!" She replied. As they took their seats Emmy said, "Now that you know a little something about my family and myself, why don't you tell me more about your family and yourself?"

"Well, let's see where I should start? My father was an attorney at law, he was well known and liked by everyone in the small town we lived in, he was known as a fair and honest man. My mother did not work outside the home, but she loved doing volunteer work, you know like at the hospital, church functions; just about anyone that would ask for help she was always there to lend a hand. My father had an older brother, but he died many years ago and he had never married, and my mother was an only child. My parents were married for many years before they had me, Mom always said she was afraid she could never have a child, because it took so long before she got pregnant with me, I was a total surprise she was thirty when I was born but today that doesn't seem so odd women seem to be having children later in life. I married right after college to someone I thought that I would be with forever, but sometimes things just don't work the way you plan them in your mind." "Are you divorced?" asked Emmy. "I will be very soon; I have signed all the necessary papers and took care of the legal aspect of it before I left the east coast. I just have to give the attorney's my address once I am settled. We never seemed to find the time to have children; my husband was also a corporate attorney in Atlanta, GA. Now that I look back maybe that was a blessing somewhat because I know that it would be harder with children involved. Boy! That sounds so depressing, my life in thirty words or less!" "You know Sid, they always say when one door closes another one opens!" "You are so right Emmy and mine has opened and here I am! Dinner is delicious!" "I am so glad you agreed to stay Sid. Have you thought of what it is you would like to do or made any type of plans in your mind?" "Now that you bring it up; I have always dreamed of having my own shop, it would carry items such as vintage jewelry, lamps, pictures, and stoneware, my hobby as always been in looking for antique stuff. But my degree from college is in business and that part of me says it's too much of a risk, yet my heart says GO FOR IT- you only get one chance at this life, and you won't know until you try."

"Sid, would you like a cup of coffee?" "Yes, thanks Emmy, cream and sugar please." "You know Sid, I may know of the perfect place for a shop, if you would like to explore that idea more, we can do some checking tomorrow and wander around town so you can see what it is like." "Yes; let's plan on that Emmy what a wonderful idea." "Sid, would you care to join Levi and I for his evening walk around the gardens?"

"Good-morning Sid! You will find coffee and pastries in the kitchen for breakfast, please help yourself I have to run to the winery office and take care of a few things, when I get back, we will head off to tour the town. See ya soon." "Thanks, Emmy." She replied.

"Oh! Hey Jed, I didn't see you standing there how are you this morning?" "I am doing good Sidney just

27

sipping my coffee and taking in the view. The coffee is there on the counter help yourself and here's the creamer and sugar." "Thank you, Jed, I just saw Emmy heading to the office, when she gets back, we will be going to tour the town." "She told me that you are thinking about opening a shop that carries vintage items, I think the folks around here would love it. You know we get so caught up in new things and always think newer is better and forget about the past."

"Jed, have you always lived here?" "Yes, my family, for several generations, have lived here and worked for the Sterling Family, they are the most wonderful people you will ever meet. I don't even feel like what I do is a job, I truly enjoy everything about this place and most of all Emmy treats her employees with such respect and, well, like we are all her family, we love her so much. Enough of that mushy stuff!

Sidney, if you decide to open a shop, I would be glad to go and help you hunt for items to sell, I think the hunting is much more fun than the find. I may even have some things stored from my family that you would like to hunt through." "That would be great Jed; I agree the hunt is the most fun. Nice talking with you Jed I guess I need to get ready before Emmy gets back." "I will have the car brought around front." "Will you be going with us Jed?" "I will be driving while Emmy gives you the tour." "Great this sounds like fun, see you in a while."

An hour or so had now past and Sidney found herself looking out over the view and daydreaming. She could picture a little shop with hardwood floors, stained glass windows in front. Huge wooden doors with a large brass door handle. A fireplace inside, with two-winged back chairs sitting in front of it, coffee, and a tea pot to one side for the customers. Each piece in the shop would have a history or at least a story to tell about where she found it, or how she recovered it.

"Sid, I'm back, are you about ready to head out on our little adventure? Sid is everything okay?" "Oh yes, I am sorry I have been daydreaming about my little shop, I was off in another world, I didn't mean to ignore you." "That is perfectly okay, I understand, believe in it as if it were so. That's the way to make things happen. Let me freshen up really quick and we will be off."

As the car left the driveway, Emmy told her how the vineyard started with only about fifty grapevines and now all you can see for miles is grapevines and when everything is in bloom it is so beautiful, it is something you just have to see for yourself. As the car made its way through Main Street, Emmy would call out each shop and the owner of the shop by name, it came natural to her she grew up with everyone and everyone knew who she was as well. "Coming up on the next corner is the New Harvest Church Sid, which is where I attend, I would love to have you visit there with me on Sunday. Jed let's stop at the coffee shop we can get a cup of coffee and walk over to Psalms Square when we are finished; that's the location of the shop I was thinking about for you Sid." "That sounds wonderful, I wouldn't mind walking and looking around a bit." As they entered the coffee shop, everyone seemed to know who Emmy was, you could hear, "Hello, Miss Sterling, and Hello Emmy how are you today? Hey, Jed, how's things going?" As they approached the counter, she could hear Emmy saying, "Lacey, I would like you to meet a guest of mine her name is Sid, short for Sidney, and Sid this is one of my dearest friends Lacey Turner she is owner of the Coffee House." "Very nice to meet you as I shook hands with Lacey, nice to meet you as well and welcome to town." "Thank you," I replied. "Hey, Jed, how are things with you? I hope okay." "Yes, Ms. Lacey things couldn't be better." "What can I get for you all?" "We would like a cup of coffee each to go please." "Coming right up."

As they exited the shop, they walked up the street and Emmy and Jed told stories and pointed to different locations and gave background on the different stores and their owners, it was a quaint place everyone seems so nice. "Sid, up a head is Psalms Square there are seven specialty shops here. One of them is the New Harvest wine and bistro shop which is owned by yours truly and next to it is a vacant shop and I own it as well. I wanted you to take a look at it and see what you thought about it, it is just around the corner." As they turned the corner, Sidney looked up and couldn't believe her eyes! The front door was tucked in a corner and the most beautiful stained- glass windows lined the front of the shop and a large shinney brass knob on the front door. She immediately flashed back to her early morning daydream about what she wanted her shop to look like; she couldn't wait to go inside. Emmy unlocked the front door and there it was just like her dream, a brick fireplace along one wall and dark hardwood floors and a mahogany counter and glass display shelves on the other wall, it almost took her breath away. "Emmy this is just like my dream, I mean my daydreaming this is how I pictured what I wanted my shop to look like, how could you have known?" "Sometimes dreams can come true." replied Emmy.

Chapter 5

As Sidney made her way down the massive staircase she was greeted by Levi, "Good morning handsome, let's get coffee and enjoy this busy day I have planned." As Sid made her way into the kitchen, she was greeted by Emmy and Madison Key has arrived, Madison is the local real estate agent. "Good morning, all." Sid replies. "Madison, I hope you were able to line up a few listings for me to take a look at, Emmy has been as kind as to allow me to stay with her. I do not want to overstay my welcome." "Non-sense." Emmy says, "I am enjoying your company it feels like new life and energy in this big house again. I have some work to get to at the winery so I will leave Madison and you Sid to your adventures around town and Good Luck!"

"Sidney, I have several homes set up and a condo lined up for you to look at, where would you like to get started?" "Let's start with the condo." Sid replies. After looking at several of Madison's listings Sid suggest they stop and have lunch. "Madison, I really thank you for helping today but I am not seeing anything that feels right yet. Buying a home is a big commitment, they always say you will know when the house is the right one as soon as you open the door 'whoever they are.'" "Yes, you are right, with my house in Atlanta I knew as soon as I stepped on the porch. We will finish lunch and look at the other two listings and see what you think."

As Sidney enters the house, Jed and Emmy are in the entry way laughing and talking. "Hi Sid, how did it go today with the house hunting? Any luck?" "Oh! Emmy, Madison showed me some lovely places, but nothing felt right to me, I couldn't picture myself in any of them. Madison is going back to her office and see if she can come up with some more listings. We will try again in a day or so. I hope it is still okay with me still staying with you?" "Speaking of that," says Emmy. "Jed and I were just talking about something we would like to show you before you look at any other homes.

On the grounds of the winery there are several cottages, Jed lives in one of them, the gardener lives in one of them, and the chef for the Bistro lives in the other one. But we also have a coach's house that was for the stables, we no longer have horse's here, and it has been empty for many years. I am sure that it will need a lot of TLC-if you want to take a look at it you are more than welcome too!" "I would love too! Emmy only if, you are sure?" "Let's go!" They made our way along the cobblestone path from the main house toward the winery then took a small turn right and continued along a path Sidney had not noticed before. Just a few feet ahead, she could see the loveliest little cottage with ivy growing up the post that held up the porch, a beautiful wooden set of French doors off to one side of the cottage.

As they stepped onto the porch and walked through the front door, they had to look through all the dust and cobwebs, they could see lights shinning in the window showing off the cutest fireplace that was in the living room and the other side could be seen in the kitchen. With a lot of cleaning and some fresh paint it would be beautiful. As they walked out the French doors, they stepped into a garden that had a lily pond and flowers all around with a garden bench to relax on. Before she knew it; Sidney was yelling with joy, "It's perfect, it fells right, I love it! Emmy how much to rent it? I would love to live here!" "It is yours and we will work out the rent later." responded Emmy. "We can get a cleaning company to help with this in a few days, you can pick your own paint colors and decorate however you like, and it's yours."

Never had Sidney ever been so drawn to someone or been at ease around people that she had known for such a short time. *I have been truly blessed by the Good Lord above.*

They made their way back up to the house and Sidney can't believe how things seem to be falling into place for her, *it's so hard to believe how low I was feeling about myself and my life and the pit it seemed to have fallen into.* But God's promise in Jeremiah 29:11, *For I know the plans I have for you, declares the Lord, plans to prosper you and not to harm you, plans to give you hope and a future*, I claim that promise.

Chapter 6

Now with the cottage cleaned up and the painters are completing the finishing touches, Sidney can arrange for her household goods to be delivered. It's hard to believe just a year ago her whole life came crashing down, from the passing of my mother to the end of a life that she had known and people that she had loved for seventeen years. *When I think back; I can hardly believe where God has me now.* Isaiah 55:8-9 says, *for my thoughts are not your thoughts, neither are your ways my ways declares the Lord, As the heavens are higher than the earth, so are my ways higher than your ways and my thoughts than your thoughts. Father in heaven, I trust your ways and I thank you for always taking care of me and directing my steps.*

Her plate has been truly full between fixing up the

cottage and getting the store set up. *Jed and Emmy have been such an amazing help to me, from helping bring stock to the store and Jed moving the furniture for me, he has picked out quite a few amazing pieces for me to sell in the store not to mention the antiques and vintage items he has found. I can't wait till this evening at dinner with Jed and Emmy I am going to ask their help in finally choosing a name for the store. As well as making plans for a grand opening date. I am so excited sometimes dreams really do come true.*

They all sit down for dinner Emmy gives thanks for the food and this day that the Lord has blessed us with. As Jed says, "Please pass the potatoes." Sidney started listing out the possible names for the store and telling the reason behind each possible name:

1. The Attic

2. Grandma's Hatbox

3. Treasure Box

4. Grandma's Attic

It used to be that every home had an attic and that's usually were you put things to store, things you no longer needed or used or things of special value you wanted to keep.

Most women would use a hatbox to store keepsakes,

love letters, notes, fried flowers, etc. Special tokens!

Jed and Emmy agreed all the names are pretty good, but "Grandma's Attic" wins hands down. "Next step," Jed said, "is to get your sign made. It has to match the ones in the Historical District of town and then get it put up at the store. I will be glad to arrange that tomorrow for you Sid, I am sure it may take a few weeks to have it ready."

As dinner draws to an end and we say our good nights, Emmy reminds Jed and Sidney that tomorrow they will go into the attic and begin to look through the items that have been stored up there to see what treasures they may find.

"Good morning to all!" Emmy says, "Grab your coffee and let's go see what secrets and surprises we can find in the attic." As she chuckles along the walk to the attic door. She swings open the door and turns on the light. "I haven't been in here for years." Everything is stacked and labeled neatly, Sidney had never seen such an organized attic before. Up front was a wooden rocking chair and a baby cradle. "Those were mine when I was a little girl."

"Emmy, may I ask, have you ever been married?" "Yes, Sid I was married to a wonderful man his name was Joshua David Sawyers he passed away from a car accident seven years ago and we never found time to have children, we just seemed content to enjoy working at the winery and spending time with each other." She could see the sad look on Emmy's face, so she decided to change the subject. "Look here is a hat box filled with cards and notes that your grandparents gave each other and there is a box of vintage jewelry. These boxes over here have some vintage hats in them how fun to wear these now. We have truly hit the jackpot! I am really getting excited about displaying and setting up the store. I have about eight weeks before the Grand Opening."

They continued for a few more hours going through different items in most of the boxes, when she noticed an odd look on Emmy's face, kind of sad. "What's wrong Emmy?" Sidney asked. She replied, "I found a small box that my mom left to me, and I thought I had lost it, but I just found it." She held the small box and left the attic. Jed and Sidney finished arranging the items so they could be loaded up and taken to the store this week.

Emmy sat quietly in her bedroom and as she opened the box, she had flashes of memories of her mother and herself when they were baking cookies at Christmas and of all the laughing, it was a happy childhood. As Emmy opened the small box inside, she finds a handwritten note that simply says, *Emmy this is the only thing that I have of any real value, and it was a gift from my mom before she died.* Emmy pulls out a simple gold locket on the front of the locket are the initials "*MG*" and the back of the locket is engraved *Love, Mom* and inside is a picture of Emmy's Grandmother. This was priceless to Emmy, she placed everything back into the box and placed the box safely into the back of her closet on a small shelf.

Chapter 7

"Wow, Sidney the cottage looks great your decorating skills are really good, you have a gift for that kind of stuff. Now that you seem to be settled in, I guess we can start planning the opening of the store and making food and beverage choices do you have any thoughts on this?" "Emmy, I have been thinking that I would like to keep it simple, I am thinking cupcakes and cookies but a little fancy not just plain old decorating and coffee, hot cider and bottled waters. What do you think about that?" "I can get Betty at the Pastry Pan Bakery to make cupcakes and cookies, I will arrange that for you." "Thank you very much Emmy for your help. We can place balloons and a banner and other fest decorations around the store."

Just then Jed came in, "Hey Sid, they have just hung the sign at the store you have to go and see it, 'Grandma's Attic'".

"Jed the sign is beautiful! Let's go in and see how the inside is coming along. I love how you have painted the shelves and set up the counter with the vintage cash register, where did you find it Jed? It's perfect! I can't wait maybe tomorrow we can start bringing in items. I am so excited; my dreams are coming to life."

Sid was up at 5:00 a.m. fixing coffee in a thermos and packing muffins she baked the night before to take with them to the store. As she headed out the door, she heard Jed say, "Here Sid let me help you with those." "Thank you, Jed. I am excited to get started today, I love staging and setting up displays, I think that's more fun than selling my items." "Sid where would you like to start?" "If you would bring in the furniture items first that will give me the main focus in each little area and then I can incorporate my smaller items. Jed, are you going to be able to move the heavy items by yourself?" "I have asked a friend of mine to stop by and give me a hand." "Oh! Is it anyone that I have met?" "No, Sid he comes into town every six months or so. He likes to come here to do his work, he is a writer, and he enjoys the slowness and quiet our town has to offer."

"Looks like he just pulled up." As Jed unlocks the front doors, "Hey! Luke come in." Just as Sidney turned around, she couldn't help but to notice a tall, brown haired beautiful green-eyed man walk through the door!

"Sid, please meet Luke Chambers, Luke this is Sidney Sharpe the store owner." As we shook hands and greeted each other, she couldn't help but to look into those beautiful green eyes! Wow-it seemed so long ago since Sidney had even noticed another man or even wanted too.

"Well let's get started, Jed can you place the cabinet over here and the rocking chair and cradle over in that corner? We need to roll out the area rugs you brought with you and let's place those in these two areas as well.

Thank you; Jed and Luke this is a great start to setting up everything. Let's call it a day with all the furniture in place I can use them as display cases and hang items from different pieces. So tomorrow I can start on the final touches to the store.

I need to get home as my household items should have been delivered, and I can start unpacking there as well. It's has been a lot of hard work, but I am having so much fun it doesn't seem like work at all."

Chapter 8

"Would you just look! She is busy as a bee in there." Emmy says as she looks through the picture window of the shop. She reaches down and grabs the door handle and walks in. "Hello! Sid, my how things are really coming together, this place is simply charming in here." "Thank you, Emmy." Sid replies.

"Do you have any dinner plans this evening, Sidney?" "Nothing special what do you have in mind?" "I would like to invite you to dinner, I am having a small dinner party for some of the folks that work in the office of the winery and Jed, of course, and I believe he is going to invite his friend Luke." "YES!" Sid exclaimed. "I had the pleasure of meeting him yesterday. He helped Jed bring in the furniture and boxes of items for me yesterday. What time should I be there?" Sid asked. "It will start around 7:00 p.m. but of course you are welcome to arrive at any time Emmy smiles. Enjoy the rest of your day."

and Emmy was out the door and on her way.

As Sidney puttered around the shop placing and arranging things oh so carefully, she found herself daydreaming about how it felt when she saw Luke come in through the door yesterday and how captivated she was by him. *I don't know anything about him is he married? Does he have children? Or maybe a girlfriend? Where does he live?* But at the same time, she remembers the pain of giving someone her whole heart and being faithful, promising to hang on through thick or thin. Just to have everything ripped away, *I don't know if it's worth that ever again.*

Where are those pearl earrings? They will go perfect with this dress. I don't want to be late to the dinner party. There they are, I forgot where I had put them in the dish on my dresser. One last look yes, everything looks good. As Sidney walks toward the main house, she notices that the sky is clear and the stars are shinning so bright, what a beautiful night it is. *Oh, good not many people are here yet. I hate being the last one to arrive.* Sidney slips in through the back door past the kitchen into the hallway where she runs into Emmy, "Hey I was wondering where you were, you look beautiful Sidney." "Thank you!" Sidney replies. "Go into the living room where everyone else is and I will be back in a moment." As Sidney enters the living room, she notices Jed and Luke speaking with some of the other guest and Jed motions for her to join them. "Sid, you look very lovely tonight would you like me to get you a drink?" "No thank you, maybe later. Sid, you remember Luke from yesterday?" "Yes, hi, how are you this evening, Luke?" "Doing very well, Sidney, thank you for asking we are talking and getting to know some of the other guest."

"Sidney is the grand opening still in three days and is everything on time?" "Yes, I am so excited I believe everything will be ready. I am so thankful for everyone's help. I couldn't have done it without Jed, Emmy, the painters, cleaning crew and you, too, Luke for your help."

Emmy enters from around the corner and announces, "If everyone would move into the dining room, we will begin serving dinner." Emmy is seated at the end of the table Jed to her right side and then Sidney in the middle with Luke beside her. "Luke, may I ask what your occupation is?" "I am a writer of sorts." replies Luke. "I write for a magazine; short inspirational stories that is why I only come to New Harvest every six months or so to have down time and focus on my writing." "I would love to read some of your work. I will see what I have with me and drop them by the store for you." "It is my turn now to ask questions, are you married? Do you have any children?" "I am divorced and no children." "How

about you Luke are you married? Kids?" "No and No."
Luke answers.

All through dinner Sidney and Luke talked and
laughed; they seemed to really be enjoying each other's
company. Dinner started winding down and people
began leaving, Sidney went to say her goodbyes as Jed
jumped in, "Luke would you mind walking Sidney to
her cottage? It is just around the corner." "Not at all
it would be my pleasure." As they walked toward the
cottage Sidney stated, "What a beautiful night this is."
"Yes, I agree such a clear and star filled night. Here we
are not a long walk." "Sidney, I really enjoyed getting to
know you better. I had a nice time tonight." "I did as well
Luke, thank you for walking me home and good night."
"Sidney, I look forward to seeing you again soon."

Chapter 9

As the sun shone through Sidney's bedroom window her alarm sounded. Sid jumps out of bed with excitement, *today is the day! I can't believe it's finally here! Now what should I wear for the Grand Opening?* Sidney rambles around in her closet and finally makes her choice of a lovely dress and boots. *This should be perfect. Not too fancy and sometimes simple is best. Now for my jewelry and I am off to open the store.*

Sidney stops in to see when Emmy and Jed would be arriving. "Emmy good morning!" "Oh, hi Sidney, how are you?" "So excited! I just stopped in to let you know I am heading to the shop to get everything set up and wanted to see what time the refreshments would be delivered." "They should be there by 8:30 this morning with the Grand Opening at 10:00, right?" "Yes, that will be perfect! Thank you, Emmy."

As Sidney unlocked the door to the shop she remembers when this was just a dream and now it's come true. She turns on the lights and looks around to get a full view of everything. It looks so good, and she is so proud of the shop. *Now I need to set up the refreshment tables before the delivery trucks get here.*

Sidney hears tapping on the glass and as she looks up and sees Luke standing in the door. She unlocks the door and invites him in. "Good morning, I didn't expect to see you this early." "Well, I wanted to bring you some flowers to place around the shop for your opening. Just then a delivery truck arrives with the prettiest arrangements of pink peonies, baby's breath, and tea roses with lush greenery. "These will look beautiful placed around the shop. One on the counter next to the register and one on each of the refreshment tables." "Thank you so much Luke! This was so thoughtful of you." "You are very welcome, Sidney, it was my pleasure." "Oh, remind me later to give you a couple of articles and stories that I have written so you can read them." Suddenly, the front door opens and there is Emmy and Jed and the bakery delivery truck. "Let's get these tables arranged! Hi Luke, I didn't expect to see you here so early." Jed said as he walked past. "Sidney, where did all of these beautiful flowers come from?" "Luke brought them. Wasn't that so thoughtful of him?"

"I believe everything is ready for the doors to open at 10:00." comments Emmy. "I believe so. We have a little time so why don't we all enjoy a cup of coffee and a muffin before we get busy and forget to eat." "That's a wonderful idea Sid," Jed replies. "I haven't had a cup of coffee yet myself." As the four of them sit talking Emmy happens to notice Sidney is wearing a simple gold locket and she comments to Sid, "What a beautiful locket, Sidney." "Thank you, Emmy, this was a gift from my birth mother. It was in her things when they originally took her to the hospital. It appears that her mother, my grandmother, gave it to her." "Oh, I see." Emmy says. "Is there anything inside?" "Yes, a picture of my grandmother."

Jed suddenly says, "It's two minutes before opening and look at the folks waiting to come inside. LET'S OPEN THE DOORS!"

Sidney said, "What an awesome first day! I so enjoyed helping people find something to treasure and being able to tell the stories of where the items came from."

"I would like to take everyone to dinner after we clean up and lock up the store." says Luke. "If everyone is up for it?" "That sounds wonderful, count me in." Sidney replies. "Jed and Emmy, how about it?" "Yes! Sounds great to us."

Chapter 10

As the sun began to rise Emmy was sitting in her kitchen with the box that she so carefully hid away in her closet. *Could there be a connection between my locket and Sidney's? They look just alike and the picture inside is the same. Should I ask her about it and show her mine? This is something I need to do. I have to find out if there is something more to this.*

As Emmy made her way down to the cottage, she kept going over how she would approach the issue in her mind. Maybe the words would come to her if she prayed. As she walked up to the door, she stopped and asked the Lord, *could there be more between Sidney and me? We both have always felt like we knew each other even though we had never met before. There is only one way to find out and here goes!*

As Emmy nervously knocks on the door, she whispers

to herself, *Lord may this go well give me the words*. After a few minutes Sidney answers the door. "Good morning, Emmy please come in. Is everything okay? You look very serious. Is something on your mind?" "Yes Sidney, let's sit down and I will explain." "No problem, you know we can talk about anything. Please, have a seat and tell me what's on your mind."

"Sidney I would like to show you something." Emmy opened her hands and put the small box onto the coffee table. She opens the box carefully and takes out her gold locket. "Emmy, you have a gold locket just mine Sidney exclaims!" "Sidney they are just alike except for the initials on the front of the lockets. Mine have the initials *MG*. Those are my mother's initials. Her name was Mary Grace. On the back of the locket, it says *Love, Mom*. As Emmy slowly opens the locket Sidney gasps! "It's a picture of my Grandmother Emmy!" With the box was a handwritten note that simply said: *This is the only thing of any real value that I have, and it was given to me by my mother.*

"Sidney, my mother Mary Grace was raised in a foster home. Remember me telling you when we first met? Her parents were killed in a car accident. This was in her personal items when she was taken to the foster home. I remember my mom always wearing the locket."

"So, do you see my surprise when I noticed yours yesterday?" "Oh Emmy, wait just a moment." Sidney left the room and a few moments later she came back carrying a small box with a small card. Sidney opens her box pulls out her locket and on the front were the initials *RG,* for Rebecca Grace. On the back it said *Love, Mom* and the note inside the card said the exact same thing.

"Emmy, do you remember me telling you that my mother was sick and that she passed? We were able to spend some time together before her passing. During that time, she told me that her natural parents were killed in a car wreck and since she was a baby at the time, they took her to the local hospital. She had been adopted by a nurse that worked there which would be the woman I came to know as Grandmother.

The locket was in the baby's belongings given to the hospital and when she was old enough my grandmother told my mother the truth and gave her this locket that belonged to her birth mother. But no other information was given to her about any possible family."

"Sidney, I believe that we should meet with my attorney and tell him our stories. Show him these lockets and have him do some investigating to see what he can turn up for us. How do you feel about that? And telling your story to him?" "I agree Emmy, I think we owe it to ourselves to find out the truth if we can."

Chapter 11

As Emmy and Sidney left the attorney's office they are smiling and laughing. "I cannot wait to share our good news with all of our friends and the town." "Yes, I think we should have a party Sidney and invite all of our friends and the local shop owners as well as the employees of the winery. This way we can share with everyone what the attorney has found out. This is such wonderful news!" "Let's have an outdoor event like a BBQ." "That sounds wonderful, Sidney." "I will get with the kitchen staff at the winery and start working on a menu. Sidney, could you take care of the invitations? Don't forget the two most important people that would be Luke and Jed?" "I won't Emmy but right now I need to go and get the store open for business. I will see you at home later today!" "Okay, Sidney, have a great day!"

"Here comes Sidney, Levi." "How was your day, Sidney?" "Really good Emmy. I had some new customers today that had driven an hour or so away. They found a few items they really liked. They are restoring a house and said they would be coming back. How was your day, Emmy?" "My day was very productive; I have the menus prepared and the wines and beverages selected. Now I am trying to decide on the desserts. I would like to have several choices but keeping them simple. How about cupcakes? They're easy for any children that may be there to handle. Or what about brownies, little apple turnovers, maybe even ice cream? Those sound perfect for an outdoor event." "Thanks Sidney! The BBQ is set for Saturday of next week." "Great, I will get to work on the invitations."

'Hey Levi, you want to go home with me for a while? You can help keep me company as I start on the invitations." "Here comes Jed, not a word Sidney, no one can know until the party!" "I won't, I promise. Hey Jed, I will see you both later, going home, Levi is with me." "See you, Sid." replies Jed. "Hi, Jed, what is going on today?" "Not a whole lot, just finished cleaning around the flower beds and the pathways. Trying to keep everything looking nice. How has your day been going Emmy?" "Well, Sidney and I are planning a BBQ for next Saturday. It is going to be a very special day, Jed! Jed, can you help arrange setting up tables and chairs and making everything look extra special?" "Of course, you can count on me Emmy. May I ask what is so special?" "Sorry Jed, everyone will find out at the same time." laughs Emmy. "I can't wait to find out what this is all about." says Jed.

"Everyone seems to be enjoying the BBQ." says Emmy. "Yes, they do!" replies Sidney. "When will we find out what all of this is about Jed?" Luke asked. "We will be making our announcement at 3:00, by that time everyone that is planning on attending should have arrived." As 3:00 approaches you see Emmy and Sidney making their way to the platform in front of the tables. As each of them take a seat you can see that they are both wearing their lockets. Jed and Luke are seated at the front table excited to finally find out what all of this is about.

At 3:00, a tall man with dark hair steps onto the platform and speaks into the microphone. "May I have everyone's attention please? My name is Dallas Rogers. I am Emmy's attorney, and she has asked me to help make this very special announcement. Before the announcement, I need to give you all a little background information. After careful research and a lot of detective work, I want to tell you a short story.

There was a couple that lived on the East coast by names of Elizabeth Grace Coats Boyd and Daniel Ray

Boyd. They had two daughters. The oldest daughter's name was Mary Grace and the youngest daughter's name was Rebecca Grace. The couple were killed in an automobile accident. The oldest daughter was sent to a foster home on the West Coast and was adopted by the Dowell Family. The youngest daughter was just a baby at the time, and she was adopted on the East Coast by the Honeycutt family. Each girl had great and wonderful lives. Each daughter had a daughter of their own and that is what today is all about. We are here to celebrate today after so many years and two different coasts. And God's special way that only he can make happen. It is my pleasure to tell you that the two daughters of Mary Grace and Rebecca Grace are none other than our own Emmy and Sidney. Emmy is the daughter of Mary and Sidney is the daughter of Rebecca Grace. They are first cousins and found their way to each other.

When you have time, you may want to ask the both of them to share with you the Secret of the Lockets."

As Emmy and Sidney stand up and their friends clap at the news, they hug each other and say, "No wonder we felt like we had always known each other."

THE END

Sharon Young

Sharon Young is from the mountains of North Carolina, the town of Mount Airy which is also known as Mayberry. She attended Mount Airy High School and graduated in 1979. Sharon worships with Mount Airy Wesleyan Church.

*For I know the plans I have for you, declares the
Lord, plans to prosper you and not to harm you,
plans to give you hope and a future.*

Jeremiah 29:11 (NIV)

CPSIA information can be obtained
at www.ICGtesting.com
Printed in the USA
LVHW022314060922
727629LV00011B/258